The HAUNTED LIBRARY

FOR BOB

BECAUSE ALL GOOD THINGS BEGIN WITH YOU—DHB

* * * * * * * * * * * * * * * * * *

I am so grateful to my agent, Sara Crowe, for coming into my life just when I needed her most, and to my editor, Jordan Hamessley, for taking a chance on an author she didn't know, and for asking just the right questions to help me deepen Kaz's world. I'd also like to thank Aurore Damant for bringing Kaz and his family to life, and everyone at Grosset & Dunlap for all their hard work on my behalf, especially Sara Corbett, Pieta Pemberton, and Sara Ortiz. When I told Sara Ortiz I wanted to do a school visit in all fifty states, she shrieked "THAT'S INSANE" in such a way that I know I'm going to love being a Grosset & Dunlap author.

Finally, thank you to my husband, Bob, for always believing in me; my children, Ben and Andy (being your mom will always be my proudest achievement), and my dog, Mouse, who lies on my feet and keeps them warm while I write.

* * * * * * * * * * * * * * * * * *

GROSSET & DUNLAP
Published by the Penguin Group
Penguin Group (USA) LLC, 375 Hudson Street, New York, New York 10014, USA

USA | Canada | UK | Ireland | Australia | New Zealand | India | South Africa | China

penguin.com
A Penguin Random House Company

Text copyright © 2014 by Dori Hillestad Butler. Illustrations copyright © 2014 by Aurore Damant. All rights reserved. Published by Grosset & Dunlap, a division of Penguin Young Readers Group, 345 Hudson Street, New York, New York 10014. GROSSET & DUNLAP is a trademark of Penguin Group (USA) LLC. Printed in the USA.

Library of Congress Cataloging-in-Publication Data is available.

ISBN 978-0-448-46242-4 (pbk)   10 9 8 7 6 5 4 3 2 1
ISBN 978-0-448-46243-1 (hc)   10 9 8 7 6 5 4 3 2

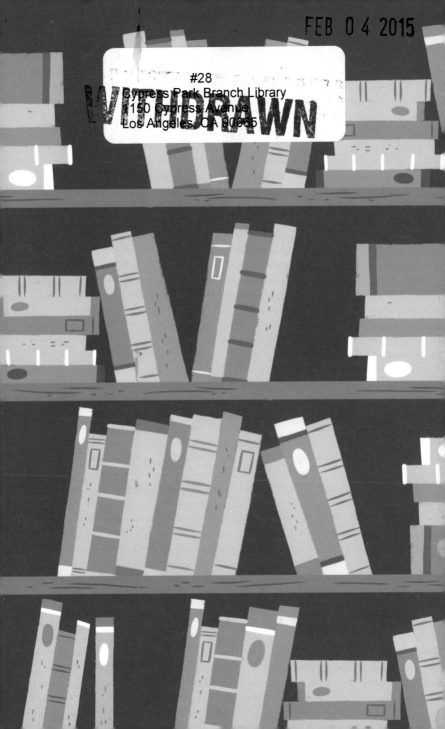

The HAUNTED LIBRARY

X

217497974

BY DORI HILLESTAD BUTLER
ILLUSTRATED BY AURORE DAMANT

GROSSET & DUNLAP * AN IMPRINT OF PENGUIN GROUP (USA) LLC

GHOSTLY GLOSSARY

EXPAND
When ghosts make themselves larger

GLOW
What ghosts do so humans can see them

HAUNT
Where ghosts live

PASS THROUGH
When ghosts travel through walls, doors, and other solid objects

SHRINK
When ghosts make themselves smaller

SKIZZY
When ghosts feel sick to their stomachs

SOLIDS
What ghosts call humans, animals, and objects they can't see through

SPEW
What comes out when ghosts throw up

SWIM
When ghosts move freely through the air

WAIL
What ghosts do so humans can hear them

CHAPTER 1

LOST IN THE OUTSIDE

Kaz floated nervously back and forth in front of the dusty classroom wall. His whole family was watching him. Mom. Pops. Little John. Even Cosmo, the family dog. They were all watching . . . waiting . . . and wondering: Would he do it *this* time?

Kaz swam back away from the wall. "I don't want to," he said in a small voice.

Everyone groaned.

"Come on, son," said Pops. "There's

nothing to be afraid of. All you have to do is take a deep breath and slide on through. Like this." Pops stuck his foot through the wall first. Then his whole leg . . . his arm . . . and finally the rest of his body.

Poof! Pops was gone.

"Woof! Woof!" barked Cosmo. The dog's tail swished from side to side as he dashed through the wall after Pops.

"Passing through is easy, Kaz," Little John said. "Watch!"

Kaz watched his little brother turn cartwheels through the wall. Little John was only six. He had already mastered most of the basic ghost skills. He could glow, wail, shrink, expand, and pass through walls.

Kaz was nine. He could shrink and he could expand. But he couldn't glow, he

couldn't wail, and he didn't like to pass through walls. He had tried it once. It made him feel skizzy.

Cosmo poked his head back through the wall. He barked twice at Kaz, then disappeared again.

"I think Cosmo is saying, 'Follow me, Kaz. Follow me!'" Mom said in a pretend doggy voice.

Kaz moaned.

Mom reached for Kaz's hand and led him toward the wall. "Let's try it together."

A solid mouse skittered into a hole in the floorboard. A solid spider danced across her web in front of the window.

"Here we go," Mom said. "One . . . two . . . three!" She passed through the wall.

Kaz yanked his hand out of Mom's grasp. He couldn't do it. He just couldn't!

Instead, he swam over to the door, sucked his body in, and shrunk down, down, down . . . until he was no larger than that old book in the corner and no thicker than one of the pages inside.

Then he dived down and slid under the door. Blowing dust mites out of his way, he swam along the hallway and into the next classroom, where his family waited.

Little John groaned as Kaz expanded to his normal size and shape.

Mom and Pops shook their heads sadly.

"You'll never survive in the Outside if you don't learn your basic ghost skills," warned Pops.

"We worry about you, Kaz," Mom said, putting her arm around him. "There are *solids* in the Outside. You need ghost skills to protect yourself from solids."

There was also WIND in the Outside. Wind that could pick up a ghost and blow him away forever.

"I'm never going to leave this old schoolhouse," Kaz told his family. "And the solids hardly ever come in here, so I don't really need ghost skills." Kaz had never been outside his haunt before, but he was way more afraid of wind than he was of solids.

"Sometimes things happen that we don't expect," Mom said. "Don't you

remember what happened to Finn?" Finn was Kaz's big brother.

"And your grandparents?" Pops added.

How could Kaz forget?

Finn, Kaz, and Little John had been playing Keep Away one day last spring. Finn often pushed his arm or leg through the wall to the Outside because he liked to hear Kaz and Little John squeal. But that day he stuck his head a little too far through the wall . . . and the wind pulled him all the way into the Outside.

Kaz and Little John had heard Finn screaming for help, but all they could do was yell for their parents and grandparents.

Grandmom and Grandpop charged through the Outside wall and tried to rescue Finn, but the wind was too strong. Finn, Grandmom, and Grandpop were *all*

lost in the Outside. Nobody knew what had become of them.

"That won't happen to me," Kaz said now. How could it? He never went near the Outside walls.

All of a sudden, there was a loud CRASH! above them. The whole building shook, and bits of ceiling rained down around Kaz.

The ghosts looked up. "What was that?" asked Little John.

"You kids stay here," Pops ordered. He and Mom swam to the ceiling and passed through to the upstairs.

Little John never liked to be left out of anything, so Kaz wasn't surprised when his brother followed Pops and Mom through the ceiling. And Cosmo followed Little John.

Kaz swam to the dirty window and

peered outside. He saw several big, yellow trucks parked in front of their haunt. One of them had a tall arm on the back. Kaz watched the arm raise a large, heavy ball into the air.

CRASH! The ball banged against the top of their haunt, and the whole building shook again.

Kaz heard Mom moan. He heard Pops groan.

"Mom? Pops?" called Kaz. "What's happening?" When they didn't answer, he swam along the rickety staircase to the second floor.

"No, Kaz!" Pops yelled back. "Don't come up here!"

Too late: Kaz was already at the top of the stairs.

He could hardly believe his eyes. Part of the ceiling had caved in. A huge

chunk of the side wall was gone. And
Mom, Pops, Little John, and Cosmo
were all floating in the Outside.

CHAPTER 2

A STRANGE NEW HAUNT

Kaz tried to backstroke away from the hole in the wall. But the wind was even stronger than he expected it to be. It *pullllllled* him into the Outside and flung him head over heels.

Above him, Mom, Pops, Little John, and Cosmo drifted higher and higher, each one moving in a slightly different direction.

Below him, the heavy wrecking ball banged into the old schoolhouse again.

Kaz watched in shock as the walls of his haunt crumbled into a pile of rubble.

He pumped his arms, kicked his legs, and tried to swim toward his mom. But the wind held him back.

He tried swimming toward his dad.

It was no use. He was powerless in the wind. They all were.

Mom cupped her hands around her mouth and yelled, "You can't fight the wind, Kaz. Just let it carry you to a new haunt. I love yooooou!" At least that's what Kaz thought his mom had said. She was so far away now that it was hard to hear.

The wind carried Kaz farther and farther away from what was left of his haunt. And farther away from the rest of his family.

Tears dribbled down Kaz's cheeks.

"Mom . . . Pops . . . Little John . . . Cosmo . . ."

He couldn't even see his haunt anymore. Or his family.

He was all alone in the Outside.

It was so bright. The sun felt warm on Kaz's head, arms, and back. Too warm.

The wind tossed and blew him over fields . . . trees . . . houses . . . a lake. Then more trees . . . a city with tall buildings. Fields again. Lots and lots of fields.

Kaz rode the wind all afternoon. Would it ever let him go?

Finally, the wind slowed and Kaz drifted down . . . down . . . down.

A big white house with a wraparound porch loomed ahead. The wind thrust Kaz straight toward the house and in through an open window.

Now that he was away from the Outside wind, Kaz could swim again. He paddled hard to the far corner of the room. As far from that open window as he could get. His whole body trembled in fear.

Once he was sure the wind wouldn't pull him back into the Outside, Kaz slowly turned and looked around. *Where am I?* he wondered.

He was in a brightly lit room. It was almost as bright as the Outside. The

room was full of bookshelves. Rows and rows of tall bookshelves, just like the library in his old haunt. Except these bookshelves didn't have any dust, and they held way more books.

Kaz swam to the next room. A sign on the door read: NONFICTION ROOM. There were more books in there. Books . . . magazines . . . newspapers . . . tables . . . chairs. And *solids*. Real, live solids.

Kaz had never seen so many solids all at once, and he'd never been this close to them before.

Some of them walked around with their feet actually touching the floor. When they walked, their feet made noise.

Other solids sat on chairs. They sat there without floating away.

What would it feel like to walk on the

floor or sit on a chair? Kaz wondered.

He didn't notice the solid woman walking toward him until it was too late. "Aaaaaaah!" he shrieked as she walked right through him. Passing through *any* solid object felt strange to Kaz. But passing through a solid *person*, or having one pass through him, felt even worse than passing through a wall or a door. It felt like the person was swimming around inside of him. Ick. Ick. Ick.

The solid woman shivered, then turned to her friend. "I just felt a sudden chill. Do you feel it, too?"

"Everyone says this library is haunted," said the friend.

Haunted? Does that mean other ghosts live here? Kaz had never met any ghosts outside of his family.

"There are always strange things going on around here," said a third solid woman. "I've heard about books opening and closing by themselves. Lights blinking on and off. And some people have even seen and heard the library ghost."

None of those solids could see Kaz.

Kaz glided into the next room. It wasn't really a room; it was more of an entryway. It had a bench in the middle and a large sprawling plant in the corner, and every wall had one or two doors. Most of those doors stood wide open, and there were signs in front of them: FICTION ROOM. NONFICTION ROOM. CHILDREN'S ROOM. CRAFT ROOM. The one door that was closed appeared to be a door to the Outside. Across from it was a wide staircase that spiraled as it went up. A black cat sat on the fourth step.

"Meow," said the cat, gazing up at Kaz through strange yellow eyes.

Finn had told Kaz that solid animals could see ghosts when they weren't glowing, but Grandpop said that was an old ghosts' tale.

The cat meowed again, then scuttled

past Kaz. It certainly acted as though it could see Kaz.

THUD! THUD! THUD! THUD! THUD!

Kaz jumped. *What is* that? he wondered, raising his eyes to the ceiling.

The thudding grew louder as an entire family of solids appeared at the top of the stairs above Kaz: a mother, a father, and a girl about Kaz's age. They made a terrible racket as they thundered down the stairs.

Kaz darted out of the way before any of them could pass through him.

The girl carried a green bag on her shoulder. She seemed to glance briefly at Kaz, but he was sure it was his imagination. Everyone knew that solids couldn't see ghosts unless they were glowing. Kaz couldn't glow even if he wanted to.

The girl followed her mom and dad to a small closet under the stairs. "But *why* can't I come with you?" she asked.

"Because we're going to be out most of the night," the mom replied as she grabbed a light jacket from the closet.

"So?" said the girl. "It's summer vacation. I can stay up. I can help you with your case." She opened her bag and pulled out a bunch of objects. "I can take pictures. I can dust for fingerprints. I can look stuff up for you on my phone. I can take notes—I'm really good at taking notes!"

The girl held up a book of some kind. Two other books fell to the floor beside her. Those books were the only things Kaz recognized in that whole pile of stuff.

"I'm sorry, Claire," her dad said

firmly. "But an overnight stakeout is no place for a young girl."

"That's why we moved in here with Grandma Karen," Claire's mom said. "Grandma needs help running the library, and we need someone to take care of you when we're out on a case."

"I don't need to be taken care of," Claire grumbled.

A grandmother solid walked into the entryway behind Kaz. She sort of reminded Kaz of his own grandmom, except this grandmom had a pink stripe in her white hair. Kaz had never seen hair like that before.

"Why don't you come with me, Claire," the grandmother said. "You can help me put away some books, and then we can decorate the children's room for Reptile Day. Won't that be fun?"

Claire did not look like she thought that would be fun at all. "I don't want to be a librarian," she said. "I want to be a detective."

"Unfortunately, you're not old enough to be a detective," Claire's dad said.

Claire's mom blew her a kiss, then opened the door to the Outside.

Kaz felt the wind and quickly backstroked away. The wind stopped as soon as Claire's parents closed the door.

"If you change your mind, I'll be in the children's room," Claire's grandma said, walking away.

Claire plopped down on the bottom

step. "I'm not going to change my mind," she said as she slammed all those strange objects back into her bag. Then she turned her head and looked straight at Kaz. "I hate being treated like a little kid! Don't you?"

Kaz looked around. *Who is this solid girl talking to? Certainly not . . . me?*

CHAPTER 3

SWIM!

The solid girl looked right at Kaz, as though she could actually see him.

Kaz glanced down at himself.

Was he glowing?

No.

Then there was no way this girl could see him.

Could she?

Kaz swam to the right. Claire's eyes followed him to the right.

He swam to the left. Claire's eyes followed him to the left.

He waved his hand in front of Claire's face and she blinked.

Kaz stared, wide-eyed. "C-can you see me?" he whispered.

"Yes."

Kaz gasped. "And you can hear me, too?"

"Of course."

"Aaaaah!" Kaz shrieked. He'd never heard of a solid who could see ghosts when they weren't glowing. He'd never heard of a solid who could hear ghosts when they weren't wailing.

This girl could do both. Was she some sort of magical solid girl?

Whatever she was, she *scared* Kaz. He turned and swam away as fast as he could.

"Where are you going?" Claire called as she held tight to her green bag and ran after him. She chased him into the nonfiction room and followed him up one row of bookshelves and down another. She could run almost as fast as Kaz could swim.

"Young lady!" An older solid lady tapped her cane on the floor. "Does your grandma let you run in the library?"

Claire slowed to a fast walk, but still she stayed right with Kaz. She followed him into the fiction room, then back through the entryway and into a brightly colored room with low bookshelves. The sign on the door read: CHILDREN'S ROOM. Most of the solids in here were Kaz and Claire's size. Or smaller. Kaz sailed right over their heads.

Oh no!

Another open window!

Kaz banked to the left and swam
back the way they'd come. Claire spun
on her heel and zoomed after him.

Kaz swam up to the ceiling. But
swimming along the ceiling in this place

was scary, too. There were round, bright
things up there that felt dangerously hot
when Kaz swam too close. Even worse,
this room had a—Kaz didn't know what
it was—some sort of whirly thing in the
middle of the ceiling. Like the Outside
wind, it *pullllled* Kaz toward it and blew

him around and around in circles really, really fast.

"HELP!" Kaz screamed, his arms and legs flailing. But who would help him? His family wasn't here.

As he spun around and around and around, he saw Claire touch a button on the wall.

The whirly thing in the middle of the ceiling slowed down. It slowed enough that Kaz could break away.

Whoa. Now Kaz felt skizzy. *Really* skizzy.

Before he knew what was happening, his stomach heaved and his insides spewed all over Claire.

"Ew!" she cried, leaping out of the way. "I didn't know ghosts could throw up."

Two small solid girls looked at Claire

like she was crazy. They couldn't see
Kaz, so they probably couldn't see the
spew on Claire's arm, either.

Claire wiped the spew away with
the bottom of her shirt as the two girls
hurried away.

Kaz's stomach felt better now. He
kicked his legs and swam to the next
room.

"Hey, stop!" Claire called, running
after him. "Come back! I'm not going to
hurt you. I just want to talk."

Kaz didn't believe her. She was a solid. His family always said: Never trust a solid.

He swam from room to room to room . . . through the entryway . . . and back through all the rooms. Again and again and again.

Claire never lagged far behind.

Kaz's arms and legs were starting to ache. He didn't know how much longer he could swim.

Just then, another ghost—a ghost man—swam out from between two bookshelves. He was about Pops's age, and he wore a fancy black jacket and matching top hat.

"This is getting painful to watch," the ghost man said as he swam alongside Kaz. "Do you want to get away from that pesky solid?"

Kaz could only nod. He was too tired to speak.

"Then follow me!" The ghost man darted out ahead.

With a burst of energy, Kaz swam after him.

Claire followed close behind.

They zipped through the children's room . . . through the entryway . . . and into a small room at the back of the entryway. The craft room. There was a table and chairs in the middle of the room, and a bunch of colorful paper objects dangled from the ceiling. They looked like birds.

The ghost man sailed under those paper birds, straight toward a wall of books at the back of the room.

Kaz moaned. He knew what that ghost man was about to do.

"NOOOOOOOOO!" Kaz and Claire
screamed together as the ghost man
passed through the wall.

Kaz screeched to a halt before his
foot touched a single book. Claire hit

the wall of books with a hard thump.

The door blew closed behind them, and Kaz was trapped in this little room. Trapped with a solid girl who could see him.

CHAPTER 4

WOOOOOOOO!

There was only one thing for Kaz to do.

SHRINK!

Kaz took a deep breath and shrank down . . . down . . . down. Then he swam up to the paper birds and tried to hide among them.

The ghost man's head popped back through the wall of books. He looked around. "Where are you, boy?" he asked.

Kaz pressed his lips together. He

knew the ghost man wanted to help
him, but he couldn't risk that girl
spotting him. So he remained quiet.

Claire moved slowly around the table, her eyes scanning every inch of the room. "Aha!" she cried, pointing at Kaz. "There you are!"

But solids can't swim in the air like ghosts can. Kaz was safe. For the moment.

The ghost man's hand appeared through the wall. "Over here, boy." He waved Kaz toward him. "She can't follow you back here."

Kaz stayed where he was.

"What's back there, anyway?" Claire asked the ghost man. "Some sort of secret room?" She craned her neck as though she could see into it through the rows of books.

The ghost man ignored her. "Hurry up," he said to Kaz. "Unless you'd rather stay with this solid girl."

No. Kaz certainly didn't want to stay

with Claire. But he didn't want to pass through that wall of books, either. Passing through a wall of books would be even worse than staying in a room with a solid girl who could see him. She'd get tired of chasing him eventually. Wouldn't she?

"Suit yourself," the ghost man said. His head and hand disappeared.

Kaz ducked behind another paper bird. Claire's eyes followed as he drifted from one bird to the next.

Claire opened her bag and slowly pulled out one of those books along with a tall, skinny object. "I'm not going to hurt you," she said again as she pulled out a chair and sat down at the table.

Kaz wasn't taking any chances. Keeping one eye on Claire, he moved slowly among the paper birds.

It was interesting how she held the tall, skinny object between her thumb and first finger and moved it across the page of her book. Kaz knew there was a word for what she was doing. That word was *writing*. Claire was *writing* in her book.

Kaz's mom and grandpop could pick up a solid piece of chalk and *write* or draw with it on a chalkboard. But it took a lot of energy and a lot of skill to do

that. More skill than Kaz or either of his brothers had.

"What's your name?" Claire asked after a little while.

At first Kaz didn't answer. But was there really any harm in letting her know his name?

"Kaz," he finally said.

"Kaz what?"

"Just Kaz."

"I'm Claire. Claire Kendall." She held out her hand for Kaz to shake.

Kaz did not swim down to take it.

"Did you just get here today?" Claire asked as she moved her writing thing across the book again.

She made it sound like he'd come here on purpose. "The wind brought me here," Kaz said.

"Today?"

"Yes." Kaz nodded.

"From where?"

"The old schoolhouse."

"What old schoolhouse?"

"I don't know," Kaz said. Was there more than one old schoolhouse in the Outside?

Kaz cleared his throat. "Can *I* ask a question now?"

Claire stopped writing. "I guess," she said, looking at him expectantly.

"How come you can see me when I'm not glowing?"

"What's glowing?"

"It's what ghosts do when we want solids like you to see us. But I can't do it, so you shouldn't be able to see me."

"Solids like me?" Claire raised an eyebrow. "Is that what you call people who aren't ghosts?"

"Yes."

Claire wrinkled her nose. "I don't think I like that word. You should call us 'people.'"

"But ghosts are people, too," Kaz said. "We're just not . . . *solid* people. Like you."

Claire started writing again.

After a couple of minutes, Kaz said, "You didn't answer my question. How come you can see me when I'm not glowing?"

Claire closed her book and laid her writing thing on top of it. "I don't know," she said. "It started a year ago. We lived in Seattle then. I just woke up one morning and I could see ghosts. I don't know why. It was kind of scary at first. There was one in our house. There was another one at my school. I tried

to tell people, but no one believed me. In fact, the kids at school made fun of me. They called me Ghost Girl."

Kaz didn't understand. Why would anyone call Claire a ghost girl? She wasn't a ghost.

"Then my dad lost his police job," Claire went on. "So we moved to Iowa. Moving here was supposed to be a 'fresh start.'" She snorted. "Some fresh start. My parents started their own detective agency, which they won't let me help with. In fact, they made me promise I won't tell anyone I see ghosts. They want me to 'act normal' here so people don't think I'm weird. But guess what? There are ghosts in Iowa just like in Seattle! So how am I supposed to act normal?" She threw her hands up in the air.

Kaz shrugged. He didn't know what was normal for solids.

"Do you think it's weird that I see ghosts?" Claire asked.

"Well . . . ," Kaz said. He did think it was kind of weird, but he didn't think it would be polite to say so.

"That other ghost who lives here says it's weird. His name is Beckett. I don't think he likes me very much."

"That's because you're a solid and he's a ghost," Kaz said.

"So?" Claire narrowed her eyes at Kaz. "Don't you think ghosts and"—she paused—"people who aren't ghosts can be friends?"

"Well . . . ," Kaz said again. *Could* they be friends? His family would say no.

Claire opened her book again. "Okay,

I told you my whole life story, but you haven't told me much of anything about you. Will you tell me your life story?"

"Are you going to write it in that book?" Kaz asked.

"Yes."

"Why?"

"Because this is my ghost book," Claire said. "It's where I keep track of all the ghosts I meet. Do you want to see it?"

Kaz still didn't want to get too close to Claire, but he was curious about her book. He expanded back to his normal size, then slowly drifted down . . . down . . . down, hovering a few feet behind her.

Claire flipped back to the beginning of the book. "This is Warren," she said. "He was my first ghost."

"You draw pictures of us in your book, too?" Kaz asked.

"Yes."

Her drawings were *good*. Better than the ones Kaz's mom and grandpop made on the chalkboard back at their haunt.

Claire turned the page. "This is Anne. She's the ghost who lived at my school in Seattle . . . and I don't know who this next one is." Claire turned another page. "She didn't tell me her name. I met her at a gas station in South Dakota."

Kaz didn't know what a *gas station* or *South Dakota* was.

The next page showed a drawing of Beckett, the ghost who had just disappeared through the wall. And the page after that caused Kaz to draw in his breath. The ghost in that picture looked exactly like his brother Finn!

Kaz couldn't speak. All he could do was point.

"I don't know that ghost's name, either," Claire said. "He wouldn't talk to me at all."

"Th-that's my brother!" Kaz said. "Finn."

Claire hadn't written very much about Finn in her book—just the fact that she first saw him on June 4 in the fiction room. That wasn't long after Finn had blown away from their haunt. Claire also saw Finn on June 6 and 9.

That was all she wrote.

Kaz told Claire all about Finn: how he passed through to the Outside and blew away.

"Do you know where Finn is now?" Kaz asked.

Before Claire could answer, the room went dark and Kaz heard a ghostly *WOOOOOOOOOO!* coming from somewhere outside the craft room.

CHAPTER 5

NO SUCH THING AS GHOSTS

laire clutched her book to her chest, grabbed her bag, and hurried to open the door. The whole library was dark.

Kaz swam into the entryway. He moved much faster in the dark than Claire did. He was used to darkness. His old haunt was always dark.

Those hot things in the ceiling lit up, and the library became bright again. A small crowd had gathered in the entryway.

"I saw it!" cried a solid boy in a striped shirt. "I saw the library ghost."

Squinting in the bright light, Kaz looked around. Solids could only see ghosts when they were glowing. But ghosts could see other ghosts all the time.

Kaz didn't see any other ghosts.

"I saw it, too!" said a solid girl in pigtails.

"So did I," said another solid boy, wearing glasses. "It was right there."

"Right where?" Claire asked as she opened her book.

"There." The boy with the glasses pointed at the air above the sprawling

floor plant, next to the spiral staircase.

"Henry," said a lady who was probably the boy's mother. "You know there's no such thing as ghosts."

No such thing as ghosts! That was like saying there was no such thing as solids.

"Maybe you saw a shadow behind the plant," the mother went on.

"It wasn't a shadow." Henry stuck out his bottom lip. "It was a ghost. It was floating above the plant, up by the ceiling. You could see right through him."

"We all heard him moan," the girl in pigtails said. "Shadows don't moan."

"And they don't turn off the lights," said the boy in the striped shirt.

Kaz drifted among the solids. The ghost man, Beckett, had passed through the bookcase and hadn't returned. So who had these solid kids seen?

Finn, he thought. Who else?

But where did Finn go?

"This isn't the first time that someone has seen a ghost in this library," Grandma Karen said in a mysterious voice.

"That's right," said a very old solid as she hobbled over with her cane. It was the same lady who had gotten mad at Claire for running in the library earlier.

"I used to own this house," the older solid said in a croaky voice. "Back before it was a library. I had a small apartment here on the first floor, and I rented out the rest of the house. We saw ghosts here all the time back then. It was hard to keep renters. When Mrs. Lindstrom said she wanted to buy the place, turn the first floor into a library, and live on the second floor, I was happy to sell it to her."

"Well, I don't believe there are any ghosts here," said Henry's mother. "Kids, let's check out our books. It's time to go home."

The old woman and all the other solids, except for Claire, walked away.

"That Beckett!" Claire shook her head as she wrote some more in her book.

"What about him?" Kaz asked.

"I don't know why he keeps coming out and—what was that word you used before? *Glow*? I don't know why he keeps glowing around all those little kids. He must like to scare them."

Kaz drifted in a circle around Claire. "I don't think Beckett is the ghost they saw. I think they saw my brother Finn."

Claire looked confused.

"The guy in your book," Kaz said,

pointing. "We were just talking about him."

"Oh, him," Claire said. "I haven't seen him in more than a month. I don't think he's even here anymore."

"Well, we know those solids—"

"Don't say 'solids,'" Claire interrupted.

"Okay, those *kids*," Kaz corrected. "We know they didn't see me, and they couldn't have seen Beckett. He went back behind that bookcase. So there's got to be another ghost here. I think that ghost is my brother Finn."

Claire shook her head. "If there was another ghost here, I would know it. Beckett's been doing this forever. Like I said, I think he likes to scare little kids."

"But wouldn't we have seen him come

back through the bookcase?" asked Kaz.

"Not if he went through a different wall."

That didn't seem possible to Kaz. If Beckett had passed through a different wall, he would've been in the Outside. No ghost ever went into the Outside on purpose.

"Well, I'm going to look around and see if Finn is here," Kaz said. He swam toward the children's room.

Claire closed her book and put it back inside her bag. "I don't think he is," she said, hoisting the bag onto her shoulder. "But I'll help you look. Just in case."

"Finn?" Kaz called as he swam up one aisle of bookshelves and down another. Claire looked high, low, and all around the room.

"Finn? Are you here?"

Kaz and Claire searched the children's room, the fiction room, and the nonfiction room.

No Finn.

"We can try upstairs if you want," Claire said. "That's where I live."

Claire led Kaz up the spiral staircase.

"This is our living room," Claire said, rounding a corner. "And that's our kitchen over there." She pointed.

Both of those rooms had strange things in them, things Kaz had never seen before. But he didn't take time to ask Claire about those things now. He was more interested in finding his brother.

Claire led Kaz down a narrow hallway. "This is my parents' office," she said, flinging open a door. "And that's my bedroom over there . . . and my grandma's bedroom . . . and the bathroom . . . and my parents' bedroom."

Living room. Kitchen. Office. Bedroom. Fiction room. Nonfiction room. Children's room. Craft room. This library had completely different rooms than the old schoolhouse had. And there was so much stuff here. *What do these solids do with all this stuff?* Kaz wondered as he paddled after Claire.

Finally, they reached the room at the end of the hall. "This is the turret room," Claire said. "It's my favorite room in the whole library." She walked to the center of the room and turned in a circle.

The room was round, not square, and very small. It had windows all around, a fuzzy rug on the floor, a small bookcase below one of the windows, and a rocking chair. The black cat that Kaz had seen earlier was curled up on the rocking chair. It looked up and meowed angrily at Kaz. Despite what Grandpop said about solid animals, Kaz had no doubt this cat could see him. And the cat clearly didn't like what it saw.

"Oh, Thor," Claire said as she bent to pick him up. "Don't be mean. This is Kaz. He's friendly." Claire waved Thor's paw at Kaz.

Kaz tried to smile at Thor, but he wasn't sure he liked Thor any better than Thor liked him.

Thor meowed again, then leaped out of Claire's grasp and padded away.

Kaz sighed. They'd searched the entire library, but they hadn't found Finn. Maybe Claire was right. Maybe Finn really was gone. And maybe Beckett had somehow sneaked past them in the craft room. Beckett probably was the ghost those solid children had seen. He was the only other ghost in the library.

Wasn't he?

CHAPTER 6

MORE
SEARCHING

There's one place we haven't looked for your brother," Claire said as Kaz drifted over to the window and gazed into the Outside. It was getting dark out there.

Kaz turned. "Where?"

"Where Beckett went. Behind that bookcase in the back of the craft room," Claire said. "I think there's a secret room back there. I've seen Beckett go back there a lot. But like he told you before, I can't

get in there. There's no door or anything."

"You think Finn could be in there?" Kaz asked hopefully.

"I think you should go find out."

Kaz agreed. But there was one problem. "I'm not very good at passing through walls," he admitted.

"Oh," Claire said. "Well, is your brother good at it?"

Kaz almost laughed. "Finn is good at everything."

"Then all you have to do is stand or"—she glanced down at Kaz's feet, which hovered a few inches off the ground—"*float* in front of the bookcase and call his name. If he hears you calling him, he'll come out. Won't he?"

"I don't know," Kaz said. "I've been calling him for an hour."

"Maybe he hasn't heard you," Claire

said. "Or . . . maybe he's hiding from you. Like a game."

Like hide-and-seek? Kaz thought. Finn loved hide-and-seek.

But this wasn't a time for games.

Kaz and Finn's haunt was *gone*. Mom, Pops, Grandmom, Grandpop, Little John, and Cosmo were all gone.

If Finn was here, he and Kaz had to stick together.

Kaz swam down the stairs . . . across the entryway . . . into the craft room . . . and all the way to the bookcase at the back of the room.

"Finn?" he called. "It's me, Kaz. Are you back there, Finn?"

Kaz waited.

Finn did not appear.

"Finn?" Kaz said again. He turned his ear toward the bookcase and listened.

He didn't hear anything.

Kaz stared at the bookcase. Passing through a wall was something almost every ghost could do. Even Little John could do it. There was no reason Kaz shouldn't be able to do it, too.

He stuck out his finger and *sloooowly* moved it toward the bookcase.

No!

As much as he wanted to, he just couldn't bring himself to step through

that wall of books. Finn would have to come to him. If he was even back there.

The truth was, Finn could be anywhere. He could be hiding in some secret room behind the bookcase. He could be hiding someplace else in the library. Or he could be miles away from here.

The entryway seemed to be the exact center of the library, so Kaz swam back in there. Then he yelled as loud as he could so Finn would hear him no matter where he was. "NO GAMES, FINN! IF YOU'RE IN THIS LIBRARY, COME OUT! COME OUT RIGHT NOW!" He paused to take a breath, then added, "I HAVE TO TELL YOU WHAT HAPPENED TO OUR HAUNT! I HAVE TO TELL YOU ABOUT MOM, POPS, AND LITTLE JOHN! AND I HAVE TO TELL YOU ABOUT COSMO!"

Kaz waited.

And waited.

And waited some more.

Finn did not appear.

Kaz's shoulders sagged.

Claire slowly walked over to him and tried to touch his shoulder, but her hand passed right through him.

"Aaaah!" Kaz darted away. "Don't do that!"

"What?" Claire asked. "What'd I do?"

"You made your hand pass through me. I don't like that. It makes me feel funny."

"Huh," Claire said. "It just makes me feel cold." She pulled out her book and wrote that down.

While she was writing, Kaz said, "I guess you were right earlier. Finn's not here. Beckett must be the ghost all those . . . *kids* saw earlier."

"Probably," Claire said. She strolled over to the big plant where the kids had said they'd seen the ghost. "But you know what? I've never actually seen him glow. I didn't see him today. And I didn't see him any of those other days, either."

"So . . . ?" Kaz wasn't sure what she was getting at.

"So, I can't *prove* that it was Beckett," Claire said. "A good detective doesn't stop until she has proof. Maybe you and I should keep working on this case until we can prove that Beckett is the library ghost."

"Okay," Kaz said with a shrug. "What do we do?"

"I don't know," Claire said. She stared at the wall behind the plant as though she might find the answer there. After a little while, she turned back to Kaz. "Detectives like my parents look for

fingerprints and stuff when they want to know who did something. Do ghosts leave fingerprints?"

Kaz looked at his fingers. "I don't think so."

"What about other evidence?" Claire asked.

"What's 'evidence'?" Kaz asked.

"Stuff that links a suspect to a crime," Claire replied. "Fingerprints. Footprints. Clothing fibers. DNA. This is where the ghost was last seen, so this is our crime scene. Beckett is our number one

suspect. So if we could find something that belongs to him, then we could prove that he's the library ghost." She walked all around the plant.

"I don't know," Kaz said. "I don't think ghosts have any of that stuff."

Claire peered closely at each of the leaves. She picked one up and looked underneath it.

"Claire?" Grandma Karen entered the room. She carried a box of—Kaz wasn't sure what all that stuff in the box was. "What are you doing?"

Claire gulped. "Nothing," she said, backing away from the plant.

"It doesn't look like nothing." Grandma Karen shifted the box from one hip to the other. She glanced around like she didn't want anyone to hear her. Then she leaned close to Claire and whispered, "Are you trying to find the library ghost?"

"Uh . . ." Claire looked at Kaz.

Kaz couldn't stop staring at the pink streak in Claire's grandma's hair.

"Listen to me, Claire," Grandma Karen said. "Ghosts like to be left alone. If you don't bother them, they won't bother you."

"Stop teasing me, Grandma. I know you don't believe in ghosts."

"What makes you think I don't believe in ghosts?" Grandma Karen asked.

Claire studied her grandma. "You mean you *do* believe in ghosts?"

"That's a conversation for another day," Grandma Karen said as she took Claire by the hand and steered her toward the stairs. "Right now, it's closing time. Why don't you go upstairs and get ready for bed? I'll be up to tuck you in as soon as I've shut down all the computers, turned out the lights, and locked the door."

"Fine," Claire said with a heavy sigh.

Grandma Karen went into the nonfiction room.

"You heard my grandma," Claire said to Kaz. "I have to go to bed."

"What's 'go to bed'?"

"It's what we say when we go to sleep. Don't ghosts sleep?"

"I don't know. I don't think so," Kaz

said. There was another word he didn't know: *sleep*.

"Huh," Claire said as she pulled out her book. "Ghosts . . . don't . . . sleep," she said as she wrote. "And . . . they . . . don't . . . leave . . . fingerprints, either. I forgot to write that down earlier."

Kaz wished he had some way to keep track of everything he was learning about solids.

"Will you still be here when I wake up in the morning?" Claire asked, stuffing her book back into her bag.

Kaz shrugged. "Probably," he said. Where would he go? If he went anywhere, he'd have to go back into the Outside. And Kaz certainly didn't want to do that.

"Good!" Claire smiled. "Then I'll see you in the morning. We'll continue our

investigation then." She trotted up the stairs.

A few minutes later, the main floor of the library went dark and Grandma Karen went upstairs, too.

Kaz was alone.

CHAPTER 7

THE LONG NIGHT

Kaz still didn't understand what *sleeping* was. Obviously it was something that took a long, long, *long* time.

How long? he wondered as he floated around the upstairs turret room. Even though he'd just met Claire, he missed her.

He missed his family even more. Kaz peered into the Outside night. He wondered where Mom, Dad, Little John,

and Cosmo were. Did they find their way to new haunts, or were some of them still blowing about in the Outside?

What about Finn? And Grandmom and Grandpop?

Would Kaz ever see any of them again?

Back at his haunt, nighttime was when the family told stories. But here in the library, without Claire for company, Kaz didn't know what to do with himself during the dark hours of the night.

Kaz drifted down the hallway. He knew Claire was behind one of those closed doors. She'd said earlier that one of those rooms was hers, but he couldn't remember which one.

He heard a strange rumbling from behind one of the doors. It sounded

like . . . well, Kaz didn't know what it sounded like. He'd never heard a sound like that before.

"Hello? Claire?" he said outside the door.

Claire didn't answer.

Kaz heard a softer rumbling from behind the door across the hall. He swam over. "Claire?" he said again. "Are you in there? What's that noise?"

Kaz sucked his body in and made himself as flat as he could. He dived down and tried to swim under the door, but the floor here was different than it had been at the old schoolhouse. It was fuzzy and thick, and it stretched all the way to the bottom of the door. Kaz couldn't swim under this door.

He sighed.

Bored, he wafted down the dark hallway . . . across the—what did Claire call this room? The 'living room'? . . . and down the stairs. When he reached the entryway, he noticed a light coming from the nonfiction room.

Didn't Claire's grandma "turn out the lights" when she went upstairs? Didn't "turning out the lights" make the library dark?

Kaz wafted over and peered around the doorway. He saw a light shining in a corner of the room. That ghost man, Beckett, hovered near the light with a book in his hands. A solid book.

Kaz stared. It wasn't easy for a ghost to hold on to a solid object. Kaz wondered how long Beckett had been doing it.

"Well, are you going to stay there in the doorway or are you going to come in?" Beckett asked as he reached out a ghostly hand to turn a page in the solid book.

Kaz was surprised that Beckett knew he was there. "How long have you been holding that book?" he asked as he swam into the room.

"About an hour," Beckett replied. "My record is an hour and a half."

"Wow." Kaz was impressed.

Beckett sniffed. "Unfortunately, I can't practice during the day with all those solids coming and going. It's difficult to even read at a table during the day. That solid with the pink stripe in her hair keeps grabbing my books out from under me and putting them away."

Kaz could see how that would be a problem.

Beckett set his book down on the table, then glided over to Kaz. "I don't believe we've been properly introduced. I'm Beckett." He tipped his hat.

"Kaz."

"Well, Kaz. I was a little surprised you didn't follow me back to my private haunt earlier. I don't extend an invitation to every ghost I meet, you know. Imagine if word got out that there was a secret place no solid could ever get into. I'd be overrun! But you didn't even want to join me."

"It's not that I didn't want to," Kaz said, lowering his eyes. "It's just . . . well, I sort of don't like to pass through walls."

"You can't pass through walls?" Beckett gaped at Kaz.

"I didn't say I couldn't," Kaz said. "I said I don't like to."

"Hmm," Beckett said. "So you'd rather spend time with that solid girl than pass through a wall."

"Well . . . ," Kaz said. Actually, he *would* rather spend time with Claire than pass through a wall.

"You don't like solids much, do you?" Kaz said.

"Nope," Beckett said, making no apologies. Kaz wasn't surprised. It was probably how most ghosts felt.

"Is that why you've been glowing in the library?" Kaz asked. "Are you trying to scare the solids away?"

"What? I haven't been glowing in the library," Beckett said. "I haven't glowed in twenty years. I don't even know if I can still do it."

"Really?" Kaz said.

Beckett shrugged. "Why would I even

want to? It's most distressing that that solid friend of yours can see us all the time. Why would I want to make myself visible to other solids?"

If Beckett wasn't the library ghost, then who was?

* * * * * * * * * * * * * * *

Kaz couldn't wait to tell Claire what he'd learned. Beckett wasn't the library ghost.

Kaz swam up the stairs, across the living room, and down the hall to where those closed doors were. They were still shut. Claire must still be sleeping. *Is she going to sleep all night?* Kaz wondered.

While Kaz floated up and down the upstairs hallway, waiting for Claire to stop sleeping, he heard a noise. It sounded sort of like solid footsteps.

Downstairs. Maybe even in the Outside.

But they were getting closer.

And closer.

Kaz floated over to the stairs to see what was going on.

The door to the Outside *slooooowly* started to open, and a shadow appeared on the entryway floor. The shadow grew larger . . . and larger . . . and larger . . . until the door opened all the way and Claire's mom and dad walked in.

"I'm *so* tired," Claire's mom said, closing the door behind them.

"It's been a long night," Claire's dad said with a yawn. He glanced toward the nonfiction room. "Looks like Mother left a light on again." He walked into the room, and the light went out.

"Hey!" Kaz heard Beckett exclaim. "I was using that!"

But of course, Claire's parents couldn't hear him. Claire's dad came back into the entryway, draped an arm over Claire's mom's shoulders, and together they tromped up the stairs.

They walked right past Kaz in the hallway.

Claire's dad opened one of the closed doors, but Claire's mom did not go inside. "I'll be right in," she said. "I want to check on Claire."

Kaz followed Claire's mom to the next closed door. The one where he had heard the softer rumbling sound. She opened the door, and Kaz floated in behind her.

Claire was lying on top of a strange box, but all he could see of her was her head. A big blanket covered the rest of

her. Thor, the cat, lay curled up on top of the blanket next to her. He gazed at Kaz through narrow, slitted eyes.

Kaz drifted closer and saw that Claire's eyes were closed and the soft rumbling sound was coming from her nose. Was this what Claire meant by "sleeping"?

Fascinating, Kaz thought.

He watched Claire's mom bend down and kiss Claire's forehead. Just like his mom used to do to him.

But Claire didn't even seem to know her mom was there. It was like her body was turned off.

Thor sat up and growled at Kaz.

Kaz flew backward.

"What's the matter, Thor?" Claire's mom whispered to the cat. "Do you see something out the window?" She turned and looked right through Kaz.

The cat leaped down from the bed and padded out of the room. Claire's mom shrugged. Then she left, too, closing the door behind her.

Once again, Kaz was stuck in a room with Claire. But this time he didn't mind. He felt less lonely when he was with Claire. And as soon as she stopped sleeping, he would tell her that he had proof that Beckett *wasn't* the library ghost.

CHAPTER 8

THE GHOST RETURNS

"That's not proof," Claire said a couple of hours later. She had finally stopped sleeping, and Kaz had just told her all about his talk with Beckett.

Kaz didn't understand. "Beckett told me he hasn't been glowing in the library. He said he hasn't glowed in twenty years. He isn't even sure he can still do it. How is that *not* proof that Beckett isn't the library ghost?"

"Because sometimes suspects lie," Claire said.

Why would Beckett lie?

Later that morning, Claire's grandma asked her to put books away. While Claire wheeled a cart of books from one room to another, Kaz wafted behind.

"Maybe there's another ghost in this library," he said as they crossed the entryway and went into the craft room. "One who isn't Beckett. Or me. Or Finn."

"Could be," Claire said. She took a book off her cart and placed it on the shelf. "But I think I'd know if there was another ghost here."

"I don't know. This place is *huge*." Kaz stretched his arms wide. "It's almost as big as my old haunt. And you're only one person. You can't be everywhere at once. Another ghost could stay hidden from you if he or she really wanted to."

"It's possible," Claire said. "But it's also possible that Beckett lied to you and he is the one who's been glowing."

Beckett charged through the wall right in front of Claire. "ARE YOU CALLING ME A LIAR?" he roared.

Claire and Kaz both jumped.

Beckett expanded to almost the full height of the room. "I . . . DON'T . . . GLOW and I CERTAINLY . . . DON'T . . .

LIE!" Kaz could almost see smoke coming out of Beckett's ears.

All of a sudden, the library went dark. And they all heard a loud ghostly *WOOOOOOOOOO!*

Kaz and Claire looked at each other.

"D-did you do that?" Claire asked Beckett. "Did you make all the lights go out?"

"Did you see me turn out the lights?" Beckett asked. "I've been floating here right in front of you this whole time."

"You still could've done it," Claire said. "I know you're mad. Don't ghosts do crazy things when they get mad?" She turned to Kaz for support.

"Crazy things like make the lights go out without actually touching the light switch?" Beckett asked. "You

have a lot to learn about ghosts, missy."

"Don't call me 'missy'!" Claire said, leaning forward.

WOOOOOOOOOOO!

"Look!" cried a voice from the entryway. "There's the ghost!"

Kaz, Claire, and Beckett all hurried to the dark entryway. They saw a ghostly figure above the plant, but it disappeared before any of them got close enough to get a good look at it.

Strange, Kaz thought. A ghost could stop glowing and then any solids in the room would think the ghost had disappeared. But ghosts like Kaz and Beckett should still have been able to see a ghost when he stopped glowing. What kind of ghost could disappear in front of other ghosts?

"*Now* do you believe I'm not the library ghost?" Beckett asked Claire.

WOOOOOOOOOO!

Several solid children ran to the entryway from the children's room. "I think the ghost went in *there*," one of them shrieked, pointing at the children's room.

"Do you see him?" asked a teenager.

"No, but I hear him! Don't you?"

WOOOOOOOOOO! The ghostly

wail did indeed sound like it was coming from the children's room.

"Must be a pretty sorry excuse for a ghost," Beckett grumbled as he followed Kaz and Claire into the children's room. "That's one of the worst wails I've ever heard."

WOOOOOOOOOO! Kaz, Claire, and Beckett looked around. The ghostly wail seemed to be coming from a large desk in the middle of the room. But Kaz didn't see any ghost.

The lights came back on and Grandma Karen said, "Don't worry, everyone. The ghost is gone. Everything is fine."

"I don't know what's going on here, Mrs. Lindstrom," said a solid man wearing a business suit. "But if these hauntings don't stop, we might have to close the library."

"Close the library? Why?" Grandma Karen asked.

"We can't have children afraid to come to the library," said the man.

"I'm not afraid to come to the library," said one of the solid children.

"Neither am I! I'm not afraid of ghosts," said another child with a toothless grin. "I like ghosts!"

The man pressed his lips together. He looked very serious. "If these hauntings

continue," he warned, "I will talk to the library board."

* * * * * * * * * * * * * * * *

"Did you hear what that man said?" Claire asked when she, Kaz, and Beckett were back in the craft room. "If the hauntings don't stop, the library might close."

"Good! I hope it does close," Beckett said.

"What? Why?" Claire asked.

"Because then I can read my books in peace, day or night, without anyone picking them up and putting them away." With that he disappeared behind the bookcase.

Claire followed him. "For your information, Beckett," she called through the bookcase, "these are *our* books, not

yours." She turned to Kaz. "If Beckett isn't glowing or wailing or whatever, we need to find out who is. We need to find the real library ghost and make him stop so that man doesn't try to close the library. Will you help me?"

"Of course," Kaz said.

But how do you find a ghost that doesn't leave any clues behind? A ghost that even other ghosts can't see?

"There you are," Claire's mom said as she poked her head into the craft room. Claire's dad was behind her. "Your dad and I are off to work."

"Okay," Claire said.

"You know, honey," Claire's mom said, lingering in the doorway, "being a detective isn't nearly as exciting as you think it is."

"That's right," her dad chimed in.

"Most of what we do is sit and wait for something to happen."

Claire's mom kissed her on the cheek, then she and Claire's dad left.

"I don't care if they won't let me help them with their detective agency," Claire said. "We've got our own case to solve."

"Yes," Kaz said, drifting back toward Claire. "And they just gave me an idea for how we might catch the library ghost!"

CHAPTER 9

STAKEOUT!

We have to do what your parents do," Kaz told Claire. "We have to watch that spot where everyone sees the ghost and wait for him to appear again."

Claire grinned. "You're right. We know where he'll show up." She grabbed her bag and went out into the entryway. "Everyone always sees him right there." She pointed. "Right above that plant." She went over to the bench and sat down.

Kaz floated behind her, keeping one eye on the plant and the other eye on the door to the Outside. Sometimes that door opened when Kaz didn't expect it. But as long as he stayed back by the bench, he would be safe from the Outside wind.

They watched and they waited. But nothing happened.

Claire opened her bag and pulled out a shiny, red ball. Kaz stared as she put it to her mouth and took a bite out of it.

"You want some?" she asked between bites as she held the object out to him.

"What is it?" Kaz asked.

"An apple. Haven't you ever tasted an apple before?"

Kaz had never tasted *anything* before. Ghosts didn't eat.

"How can you throw up if you don't eat?" Claire asked. "What are you throwing up?"

Kaz shrugged. "My insides."

Claire and Kaz remained in the entryway for the rest of the afternoon. Lots of solids walked through. Some of them, like Grandma Karen, walked through more than once.

But no ghosts wafted through.

The next day, Kaz and Claire watched the entryway again.

Still no ghosts. But the lady who used to own the house came in. Kaz wasn't sure she saw Claire sitting on the bench, even though Claire wasn't a ghost. The lady held her cane in one hand and a magnifying glass in the other. She hobbled over to the plant and peered through her magnifying glass.

Kaz and Claire glanced at each other. *What is that lady doing?*

Claire cleared her throat.

"Good heavens!" the lady said. "You scared me half to death."

"Sorry," Claire said. "What are you doing?"

"I lost an earring when I was in here the other day," the lady said. "I'm trying to find it. But I'm too old to get down on the floor."

"I'm not," Claire said, dropping to her hands and knees. "Maybe I can find it for you."

Kaz swam along the floor beside her.

"What does your earring look like?" Claire asked.

"It's round, with blue and silver jewels in it," the woman said.

"Is this it?" Kaz asked, hovering over a small, sparkly object.

Claire grabbed the object. "Found it," she said, handing it to the lady.

"Oh, thank you, dear," she said.

"Well," Kaz said at the end of the day, "we may not have solved the case of the library ghost, but we solved the case of that lady's missing earring."

On the third day, Grandma Karen said, "What are you doing, Claire? Why do you sit here day after day? If you don't want to work in the library, why don't you go outside and play?"

"I don't like to play outside," Claire said.

"Nonsense. Everyone likes to play outside. You could use some fresh air."

"I'll think about it," Claire said. But she stayed right where she was.

Later, Beckett joined Kaz and Claire in the entryway. "Why *do* you two sit

here day after day?" he asked. "Don't you find it dreadfully dull?"

"We're waiting for the library ghost to appear," Claire said.

"What makes you think that he or she is going to appear while you're sitting here?"

"What do you mean?" Claire asked. "Why wouldn't he appear while we're sitting here?"

"Because the 'ghost' probably isn't a *real* ghost like Kaz and me," Beckett said. "It's probably a solid *pretending* to be a ghost."

"You know I hate that word, Beckett," Claire said, glaring at him.

"Wait, Claire," Kaz said. "Beckett could be right. What if the 'ghost' isn't really a ghost?"

Claire thought about it. "Then he

won't come out while I'm sitting here," she said finally. "Because he won't want *me* to see him. He won't want me to know he's not a real ghost."

"Right," Kaz said.

"We have to hide," Claire said, glancing all around, her eyes fixing on something at the top of the stairs. "And I know the perfect hiding place. Follow me!"

Kaz followed Claire as she raced up the stairs. She went to the cabinet at the top of the stairs and flung open the doors.

The cabinet was mostly empty, except for a couple of blankets on the floor.

"I hide in here sometimes when I want to spy on my parents," Claire told

Kaz. "But I'm not sure it's big enough to hold both of us."

"Sure it is," Kaz said. "I can shrink, remember?" He sucked his body in and shrunk down . . . down . . . down . . . until he was small enough to float in a corner of the cabinet.

Claire grinned. "It is so cool that you can do that!" She tossed her green bag into the cabinet and then crawled in after it. She closed the doors, but the cabinet wasn't dark. Little circles of light shined in through several holes in the back of the cabinet.

"Look! You can see the whole entryway if you look through one of these," Claire said, pressing her eye against one of the holes.

"Did you put these holes in here?"

Kaz asked as he looked through another hole.

"Me? No!" Claire said. "But they're good for spying, aren't they? I bet whoever put them here was a detective like us. Maybe this was their secret hideout."

"Could be," Kaz said.

Kaz and Claire watched. And waited. And waited some more.

Claire shifted position. "This is starting to get kind of boring," she admitted after a while. "Good thing I've got stuff to do in here." She opened her bag and pulled out a strange object.

"What's *that*?" Kaz asked.

"It's a flashlight," Claire said. She pushed a button on the side of the object, and light poured out of it.

Kaz squinted against the brightness. "What do you do with it?"

"Lots of things," Claire said. "Mostly you use it to light up dark places like this."

Kaz peered into her green bag. "Is there anything you don't carry in there?"

Claire laughed. "This is my detective bag. A good detective is prepared for *everything*," she said. "Let me show you what else you can do with a flashlight." She held two fingers up and shined the flashlight on the side of her hand. "Look!"

Kaz saw a circle of light shining on the wall of the cabinet. But in the center of the circle was a dark shape that looked like a bouncing rabbit.

"It's my shadow," Claire said. "I can make an alligator, too." She changed the position of her hands.

"What's an alligator?" Kaz asked.
He'd never seen a figure like the one
Claire projected onto the cabinet wall.

"It's a reptile that lives in Florida,"
Claire explained.

Kaz didn't know what Florida was,
either.

"And here's a horse," Claire said. "It's
all in how you hold your hand."

Kaz was fascinated.

"Do you want to try?" Claire asked. "Hold your hand like this and you can make a horse, too."

Kaz bent his fingers like Claire's and tipped his wrist back. Claire shined the flashlight on his hand. But no shadow appeared.

"Oh," Claire said, disappointed. "Ghosts don't have shadows. I should've known that." She pulled out her book and wrote it down.

"Oh well." Kaz shrugged. He still enjoyed watching Claire make animal shadows with her hand, even if he couldn't do it, too.

Claire shifted position again. "My legs are getting sore," she said, switching off the flashlight. "I don't think the library ghost is going to show up

tonight, either. Maybe we should give up."

But just as she said that, the lights in the library went out. And Kaz and Claire heard that same ghostly *WOOOOOOOOOO!* They each peered through holes in the cabinet and saw a figure dart across the dark entryway below them.

CHAPTER 10

PARTNERS

Claire grabbed the flashlight, which was still switched off. She flung open the cabinet and tore down the stairs in darkness. Kaz swam behind her.

Beckett hovered above the door to the Outside. He wasn't glowing, so Kaz and Claire could see him, but no one else in the library could.

Another ghost appeared above the plant. The same place Kaz, Claire, and Beckett had seen it before. Except up

close it didn't look much like a ghost. It looked like . . . *a cloud of white fog.*

A dark solid figure tiptoed away from the "ghost," toward Kaz and Claire.

"Aha! Caught you!" Claire said. She switched her flashlight on, and a bright light shined on . . . Claire's grandma!

"I knew it," Beckett said in a bored voice. "A solid pretending to be a ghost."

At that exact moment a small solid boy cried from the children's room, "GHOST! I see the library ghost!" He pointed to the fog behind Grandma Karen and Claire.

Grandma Karen turned. She put her hands to her cheeks. "I see it, too!" she said as several other solids came running.

But she was only pretending! There was no ghost. Kaz and Claire knew this, even if the other solids didn't.

Grandma Karen shook her head at Claire and put her finger to her lips.

The foggy "ghost" disappeared.

"Where did he go?" asked a solid boy in a red shirt. He stomped his foot. "Why does that ghost always disappear before I get to see him?"

"I don't think the ghost wants too many people to see him," Grandma Karen said. She opened the door under the stairs and flipped a switch. The entryway grew bright again.

"Maybe we'll get to see the ghost the next time we're at the library," said a solid girl as she and her mom headed for the door.

"Grandma!" Claire said, once everyone had left the library. "*You're* the ghost."

Grandma Karen blushed. "Yes," she admitted. "I am."

"But why?" Claire asked. "Why are you pretending to be a ghost? And *how*? How did you make the ghost appear? How did you make it wail? How did you make all the lights go out? How did you do it all at the same time?"

"Oh my. So many questions," Grandma

Karen said with a nervous laugh. "I'll answer your questions if you promise not to tell anyone what I'm about to tell you. Do you promise?"

Claire nodded.

"Okay," Grandma Karen said, leading Claire over to the plant. "First, there's a fog machine hidden in that pot. That's why I didn't like you poking around here the other day." She pushed some of the dirt aside until a red button appeared. "Here's the button to turn it on."

Claire pushed the button and the "ghost" rose up above the plant again.

"What about the lights and the sound?" Claire asked. "How did you make all the lights go out, and how did you make the ghost sound?"

Grandma Karen led Claire to her desk

in the children's room. Kaz and Beckett floated along behind.

"Remote control," Grandma Karen said, opening the top drawer. She pointed. "Don't push this button. That's the one that turns out all the lights. But you can push the other button."

Claire did.

They all heard the ghostly WOOOOOOOOOO! coming from a box on Grandma Karen's desk.

"I told you that didn't sound like a real ghost," Beckett grumbled. Then he swam away.

"But why, Grandma? Why are you doing this?" Claire asked. "Aren't you worried about that man closing the library?"

Grandma Karen smiled. "No," she said. "I think people like the idea of a ghost in the library. In fact, they might come to the library more often because they want to catch a glimpse of the ghost. Mr. Argen might complain to the library board, but the board will never vote to close the library."

"Are you sure?" Claire asked.

"I'm sure," Grandma Karen said.

* * * * * * * * * * * * * * * *

Later, when Kaz and Claire were talking in the turret room, Kaz said, "I guess we solved the case of your haunted library."

"I knew we would," Claire said happily. She peered at Kaz. "You don't look very happy that we solved the case."

Kaz shrugged. "I'm happy that we solved the case, but I miss my family. And I miss my old haunt."

"Well, you can stay here in the library as long as you want," Claire said. "Maybe the library can be your new haunt."

"Maybe," Kaz said. "And thank you. That's very nice of you. But I wonder if I'll ever see my family again?"

Claire rocked back and forth in the rocker. "I was thinking about that," she said.

"You were?"

"Yes. Well, about that *and* about how we solved the case of the library ghost." Claire stopped rocking and turned to Kaz. "I think you and I should start our own detective agency. It would be like my mom and dad's, except we'd solve *ghost* cases. We could call ourselves C & K Ghost Detectives, for Claire and Kaz. What do you think?"

She looked really excited about the idea.

"But your parents said you're too young to be a detective," Kaz said.

"I'm *not* too young," Claire said firmly. "And neither are you. Think about it. If we become ghost detectives, we could find your family."

"Really?" Kaz brightened at the thought. In fact, he almost glowed.

"Yes. If someone has a ghost in their house, they'll call us and then we can go find out if it's someone from your family."

Kaz liked that idea. He liked it a lot.

"For sure we'll make a ton of money," Claire said.

"Money? What's that?" Kaz asked.

"You don't know what money is?" Claire gaped at him.

"No."

Claire laughed. "You have a lot to learn about the world outside your old haunt, Kaz. But don't worry. I'll teach you everything you need to know." Claire held out her hand. "Partners?" she asked.

Kaz rested his ghostly hand right next to Claire's solid hand. "Friends," he said.

BY EDGAR AWARD WINNER DORI HILLESTAD BUTLER

The HAUNTED LIBRARY

THE GHOST IN THE ATTIC